The Great BUFFALO RACE

How the Buffalo Got Its Hump

A Seneca Tale Retold by

BARBARA JUSTER ESBENSEN

Illustrated by

HELEN K. DAVIE

Little, Brown and Company
Boston   New York   Toronto   London

Note to the Reader

It may seem surprising to find a buffalo legend originating with the Seneca, who were part of the Iroquois Nation, a tribal culture of the eastern woodlands. But around a thousand years ago, wandering buffalo herds from the Great Plains crossed the Mississippi River and worked their way east. Some roamed all the way to the Atlantic coast. Others went northward to the Canadian forests.

In addition, Iroquois war parties from upper New York State fought campaigns that took them to the Mississippi and beyond. So they were familiar with the buffalo herds farther west on the grassy plains, as well as the bands of buffalo in the eastern forests.

This old tale, like all Seneca legends, was told during the long winter nights by Seneca storytellers. It was taken down by Arthur C. Parker, whose Seneca name was Gawaso Wanneh, and it can be found in his collection *Skunny Wundy*, where it is entitled "The Buffalo's Hump and the Brown Birds" (Doubleday, 1926).

The patterns and costumes found throughout the illustrations were inspired by traditional beadwork and clothing found in books on the Iroquois as well as at the American Museum of Natural History and the American Indian Museum, Heye Foundation, both in New York.

Every year in those far-off times we only dream about now, the Tribe of Buffalo would gather together to choose a day for the race to new fields. Every year the buffalo would chew the juicy green grasses until only the shortest stems remained. When this happened, they would prepare themselves to race to the tall, lush grasses that grew in their other fields over the far horizon.

In those days, the winner of the race would become the grand chief over all the vast herd. The race always began at sunrise and ended at sunset. Soon it would be time once again to decide when to go.

But the thunder god had not poured down his gift of rain for many months.

And the herd had watched their once-grassy plain grow so dry and withered that there was hardly a blade left worth eating. Only dust and stubble remained under their hooves.

Then one day, the buffalo sensed something new on the wind that blew toward them from the western lands. One by one, they raised their huge heads and breathed into their nostrils the wet, green scent of rain and grass. And one by one they stamped and snorted, restless to race out to the fields where they would find good grazing once again.

But Old Buffalo held back his followers. "Be patient. The rain will come. That rain we now feel on the wind is far, far away. At the setting of the sun, when the race is ended, we would still not be standing beneath the wet drops." Dust rose like a whirlwind around him, and the other buffalo fell silent.

But Young Buffalo pushed his way out of the crowd. He had a dangerous fire in his eye.

He turned to his followers and snorted, "Do not listen to the old one. We will not obey him. We will leave tomorrow at sunrise for the green grasses that await us far to the west. Tomorrow at sunrise!"

And he wheeled around to face Old Buffalo, who had been chief for many years. The old one met him now with lowered horns and eyes that rolled white with fury.

"I say we will not go!" the old chief fumed, stamping his hooves with each word. "Even if we managed to run so far by sunset, it would be wrong to do so. Out there are other buffalo tribes. They, too, have waited for relief from the sun blazing down on their own dusty, barren lands. We must not take those new grasses from them. The rain will make its way to our own lands. Be patient. The time for the race to new fields is not yet here."

"And I say we leave at sunrise!" declared Young Buffalo. "But we can settle this with a contest," he added, glancing slyly at his followers. "We shall wrestle. If you throw me onto my back, Old One, we will stay. If I throw you, we shall leave at first light tomorrow." He turned again to his followers, who were snorting and pawing the dust.

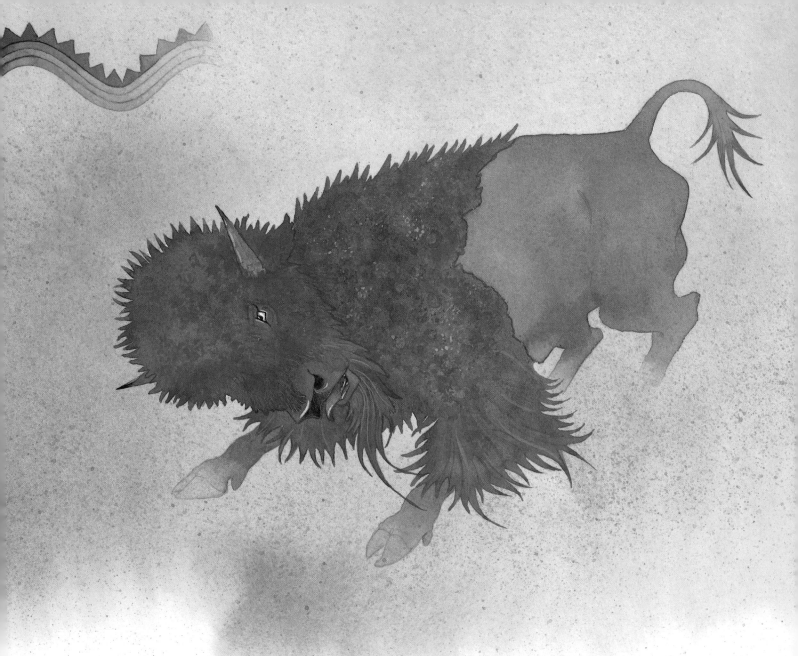

"By sunset on the morrow," Young Buffalo announced, "someone among us will be the chosen chief of all buffalo. A new chief. A younger, stronger chief. I feel in my bones that I already know his name!" He tossed his shaggy head and rolled his eyes at his cheering buffalo kin. "And we will be filling our mouths with the fat, green grasses that have sprung up under the rain," he added, glaring at Old Buffalo.

The old chief hesitated, but he saw that the herd was determined to settle this once and forever. He accepted the challenge.

Young Buffalo and Old Buffalo wrestled. The air was dark with the sound of their heavy breathing. They lunged and bellowed. Their curved horns clattered as the two fighters ran the sharp tips hard against each other. They pushed and twisted their shaggy bodies this way and that.

Then, without warning, one of Young Buffalo's brothers edged out of the watching herd, lowered his horns, and charged at Old Buffalo from the other side. Now it was two against one! Before the old chieftain could defend himself against this treacherous attack, Young Buffalo's brother jabbed a horn into him.

The old chief spun around with a terrible snort, and Young Buffalo, seeing his chance, lifted the old chief into the air and tossed him over onto his back.

A terrific roaring shout came from the throats of Young Buffalo's kin. "Tomorrow we go!"

The old chief picked himself up, his eyes gleaming with anger.

"I will keep my word, for my word is my honor," he said. "But Young Buffalo has shown that he cares not for an honorable win. His victory was brought about through treachery. Beware that he does not trick all of you as well."

"Fair is fair in a fight," retorted Young Buffalo, winking at his followers.

"Not in the eyes of Haweniyo, the Great Spirit," said the old chief. "And you know well that if one of us makes a grave error, all will suffer."

"Too much talk!" bellowed all the young buffalo, eager to win the race to find the rain. Each of them was impatient because each expected himself to be the winner and new chief. "The important thing is that you lost. We leave tomorrow."

When the first light glowed in the morning sky, the buffalo divided themselves into three herds.

The first, followers of Old Buffalo, were the cautious ones. They were not happy to compete in the western lands with others of their kind who had waited so long for the rains to come. However, they trusted their chief to know what was best, and so they followed his lead.

The second group was the vast tribe who followed Young Buffalo. They wanted action, and they were running for the glory of becoming chief. Little did it matter to them that other herds on the western plains needed green grasses, too.

A third group had remained quietly in the background while all the arguments and ferocious wrestling had been going on. Their leader was Old Buffalo's son, a wise youngster called Brown Buffalo.

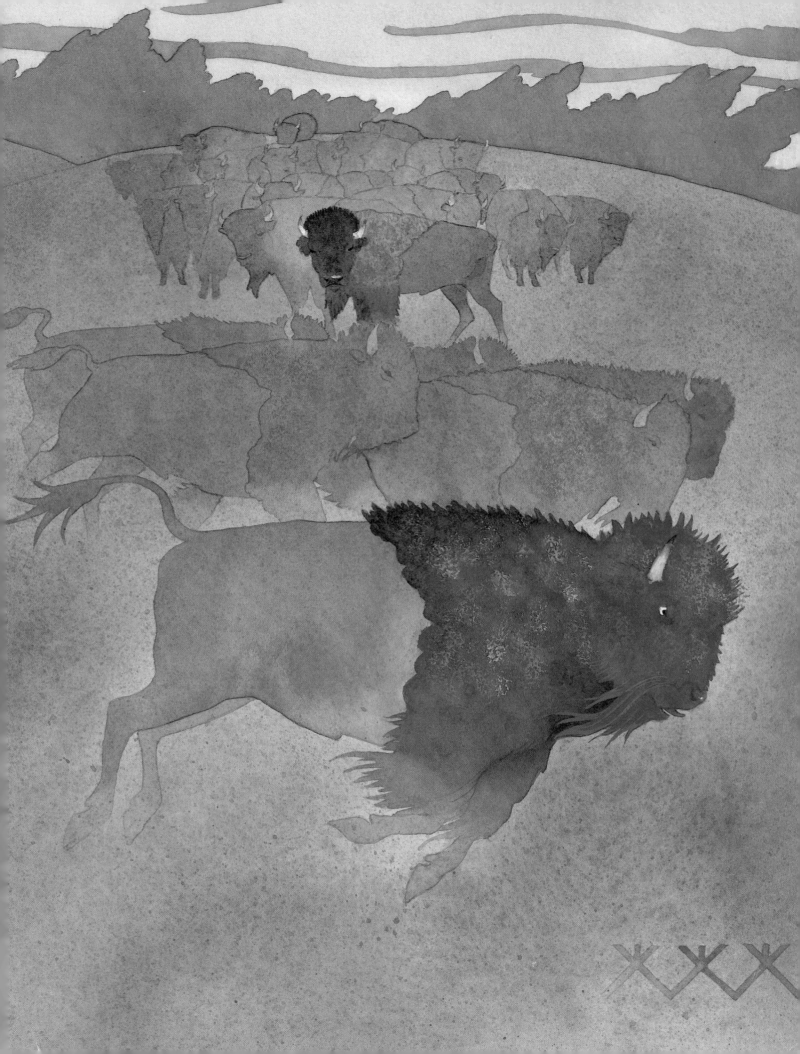

Now, as the sun's red brow rolled up over the horizon, Old Buffalo shouted, "Follow me!" and his followers thundered away behind him, taking a winding way that led through short grass. This made running easy for there were no nests or small animals to avoid in the short grass.

"Follow me!" echoed Young Buffalo, and all the impatient buffalo galloped away with him toward the western horizon. They charged straight ahead, tearing through the tall, dry, sunburnt grasses where many small birds and animals lived.

"And we will stay here, as common sense tells us to do," said Brown Buffalo to the group who remained. "Rain will come to us, and we will have grass, just as my father, Old Buffalo, told us. For the first time in my life I will not follow my father where he leads."

Those who stayed behind with Brown Buffalo felt the ground tremble as the other two herds stampeded westward on their two separate courses. Brown Buffalo and his followers sweltered in the blazing sun and nibbled what little dry grass they could find in the cracked earth.

Young Buffalo and his herd rumbled across the plains, trampling everything in their headlong race toward the rainy fields. They felt more powerful than any creature under Haweniyo's great eye. They did not care about those who were weaker than themselves. Whole flocks of homeless brown birds flew up. The birds screamed and wheeled in the dusty air as thousands of buffalo hooves tore through the clumps of brittle grass, crushing nests and eggs and anything else that lay in their path.

Old Buffalo and his herd thundered over the short grass and sped along the winding route, always racing westward.

The sun rose higher and higher, scorching the ground. The buffalo began to drop, one after another, from thirst and exhaustion. Hundreds fell to the earth, too tired to run any farther. Soon only Old Buffalo and Young Buffalo were still in the race.

They ran and ran until finally their paths merged and they were running side by side to the place where the sun falls off the edge of the plain.

Now it disappeared, leaving only a red smear in the evening sky. The race was over. They looked all around them, and then, with rolling eyes and heaving sides, they turned to stare at each other. The race was over, yes. But everywhere they looked, the grass was dry and sparse. Not a blade of green as far as their hot, tired eyes could see. They had not reached the rainy fields after all.

The sky darkened, and then it lit up as a great shimmering cloud appeared. A figure, clothed in light and streaming with a million stars, stepped out of the cloud and descended to earth.

Both buffalo leaders stared at the figure, awestruck.

Haweniyo, the Great Spirit, spoke:

"Foolhardy buffalo, you have slain your followers. They have died because you asked them to follow you, and now there is not one left. You were seeking a land blessed by fine rain and rich grass. Behold! It is there, on the eastern horizon, in the fields where you began this foolish race."

And they heard, far off to the east, the rumble of thunder and smelled the unmistakable scent of rain.

"Your own son, Brown Buffalo, learned much from you, Old One, and he followed your teachings even if you did not. He is there in the green fields with the other wise buffalo who stayed with him. He is chief now and guides all that remains of your tribe.

"Now step forward and receive your punishment, that all buffalo may remember this day."

The two buffalo stepped forward. As they did, the Great Spirit struck them over their shoulders with his spear. Immediately, a hump appeared upon the massive shoulders of each animal. It would mark their disobedience forever.

"You, Young Buffalo, why did you destroy all those small brown birds and their young?"

"My herd and I thought it good sport to rush over them, to crush the eggs and to see all the weak, confused birds fly up as we passed by."

"From this day forth, you will look where you step," said the Great Spirit. "All buffalo who exist today, and all who will be born in the future will, by this token, remember!"

And with those words, Haweniyo, the Great Spirit, stepped upon Young Buffalo's head and pushed it toward the ground.

"Now you will be aware of all the lowly, helpless ones that live and move beneath your feet."

Then Haweniyo lifted his hand and spoke to Old Buffalo. His voice was full of sadness.

"Old Buffalo, once you were wise. Even in this foolishness, you gave good advice. But you did not heed your own words, and you did not lead like a true wise one.

"I now transform you into the White Buffalo of the clouds. Whenever there is danger ahead, you will appear in the heavens to warn your kind."

Then he touched Old Buffalo with his spear, and the old chief became ash white and flew straight into the night sky, to live among the clouds forever.

The Great Spirit turned again to Young Buffalo. "You were impatient and did not listen to reason. The green earth you sought is now far to the east, where Brown Buffalo leads his herd at this very moment. You are a destroyer of birds. So from this day forward, those small brown birds shall depend upon buffalo for food and protection. Even now, your kinsmen in the east find themselves surrounded by brown birds who will live with them for all the years to come.

"As for you, I will transform you into Red Buffalo of the under-earth. Be gone!"

And Young Buffalo became red and sank deep into the earth, where Haweniyo sends those who displease him with their thoughtless and cruel behavior.

The next morning, Brown Buffalo stood among the lush green grasses that now grew thickly around him. He looked at his tribe. To his surprise, he saw humps on every shoulder. He saw that the heavy heads of all of his kinsmen, and his own head as well, were bent nearly to the ground.

And all around the herd flew hundreds of friendly brown birds that picked at the grasses and flew up to ride upon the back of every buffalo. So it was on that day so long ago, and so it is today, and so it will be forever.

To all who love and cherish these ancient tales and
who wish to make them come alive for the children of today

B. J. E.

For Barbara J. Esbensen
Thank you for sharing your gift – the love of words

H. K. D.

First Edition

The Great Buffalo Race is a Seneca tale retold from "The Buffalo's Hump and the Brown
Birds," in *Skunny Wundy*, by Arthur C. Parker, copyright by George H. Doran Company,
published by arrangement with Doubleday, 1926.

Library of Congress Cataloging-in-Publication Data
Esbensen, Barbara Juster.
  The great buffalo race : how the buffalo got its hump : a Seneca tale /
retold by Barbara Juster Esbensen ; illustrated by Helen K. Davie.
    p.   cm.
  Summary: A retelling of the Seneca legend in which the buffalo receives
its hump from the Great Spirit.
  ISBN 0-316-24982-3
  ISBN 0-316-91156-9 (UK pb)
  1. Seneca Indians — Legends. 2. Bison, American — Folklore.
[1. Seneca Indians — Legends. 2. Indians of North America — Legends.
3. Bison — Folklore.] I. Davie, Helen, ill. II. Title.
E99.S3E73   1994
398.2'089975 — dc20
[E]   92-23410

10 9 8 7 6 5 4 3 2 1

SC

Published simultaneously in Canada by Little, Brown & Company (Canada) Limited
and in Great Britain by Little, Brown and Company (UK) Limited

Printed in Hong Kong